"Stella," whispered Sam, "are you sleeping?"
"Yes," answered Stella. "Aren't you?"

"No, said Sam. "I can't sleep."
"Why? Are you having a bad dream?"

"No," answered Sam. "I can't sleep without Fred."

"Where is he?" asked Stella.
"I don't know."

"Did you look under your bed?"

"He's not there," said Sam.

"Fred sneezes when he's under the bed."

"Maybe he's outside," said Stella.

"It's too dark outside," said Sam.
"Fred is afraid of the dark."

"Look in the closet," said Stella.
"A monster lives in that closet," said Sam.
"Fred would never go in there."

"Go to sleep, Sam," yawned Stella.
"I can't sleep without Fred," said Sam.

"Why don't you try counting sheep?" asked Stella.
"Sheep? What sheep?"

"First you close your eyes," said Stella.
"And imagine hundreds of sheep. Then you count them."
"I can only count to three," said Sam.

"I guess we'll have to look for Fred," sighed Stella.
"I know he isn't downstairs," said Sam.
"Fred doesn't like those strange noises."

"That's only the clock ticking, Sam. Come on."

"Maybe he's in the living-room," said Stella.
"Behind the couch or under the big armchair."

"Fred never goes near that chair," said Sam.
"He thinks it looks like a giant toad."

"Look!" cried Sam. "A ghost!"

"That's the moon, Sam."

"If Fred was here," said Sam, "he would bark at the moon."

"Fred never barks," said Stella.
"Yes, he does," whispered Sam.
"Fred barks when he's afraid."

"I'm tired, Sam. We'll look for Fred tomorrow."
"Will we get up early?" asked Sam.

"We'll get up with the birds," answered Stella.

"Birds? What birds?"

"Come on, Sam," sighed Stella.

"Stella!" cried Sam. "I found Fred!"
"Where?"

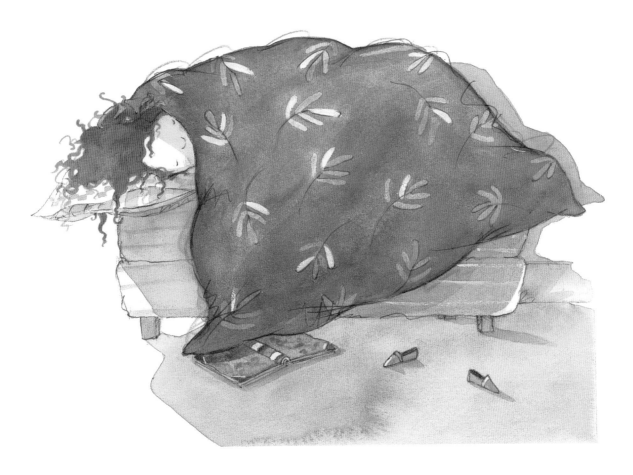

"He was sleeping under my quilt," said Sam.
"Good!" yawned Stella. "Let's sleep too."

"Stella?" whispered Sam. "I still can't sleep."
"Why not?"
"Fred is snoring too loudly," said Sam.

"Good night, Sam," sighed Stella.